Island
~ of ~
Sodor

Barrow

Skarloey

Rheneas

Vicarstown

Ballahoo

Glennock

Norramby

Cros-ny-Cuirn

Crovan's
Gate

Kellsthorpe

Rolf's
Castle

Kirk Ronan

Thomas the Tank Engine & Friends™

CREATED BY BRITT ALLCROFT

Based on The Railway Series by The Reverend W Awdry.
© 2008 Gullane (Thomas) LLC.
Thomas the Tank Engine & Friends and Thomas & Friends are trademarks of
Gullane (Thomas) Limited. Thomas the Tank Engine & Friends & Design is Reg.
U.S. Pat. & Tm. Off.
HIT and the HIT logo are trademarks of HIT Entertainment Limited.

www.randomhouse.com/kids/thomas
www.thomasandfriends.com

Library of Congress Cataloging-in-Publication Data
Halloween in Anopha / illustrated by Richard Courtney. — 1st ed.
    p.   cm. — (Thomas & friends)
"Original holiday story based on The Railway Series by The Reverend W Awdry."
Summary: Thomas is excited about the Halloween party being planned at the
quarry in Anopha, but as one thing after another delays him it seems that he
will never get there in time.
ISBN 978-0-375-84413-3
[1. Railroad trains—Fiction. 2. Halloween—Fiction. 3. Parties—Fiction.]
I. Courtney, Richard, ill. II. Awdry, W. Railway series.
PZ7.H1587 2008   [E]—dc22   2007040843

MANUFACTURED IN CHINA
10 9 8 7 6 5 4

HiT entertainment

THOMAS & FRIENDS

Halloween in Anopha

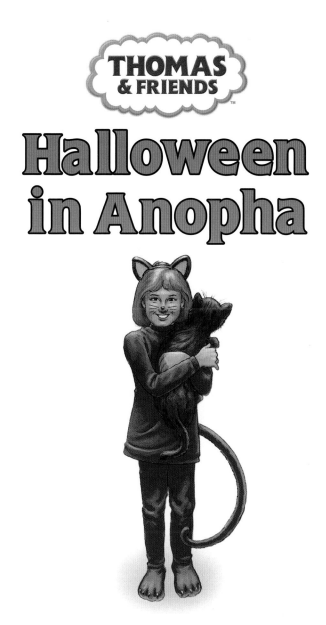

Based on The Railway Series
by The Reverend W Awdry

Illustrated by Richard Courtney

RANDOM HOUSE 🏠 NEW YORK

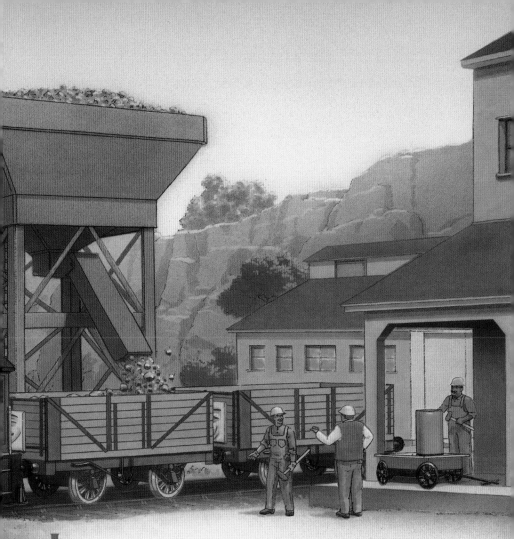

It's the end of October and the trees of Sodor are wearing coats of bright red, yellow, and orange.

Anopha is a small town with a big quarry near Ffarquhar. Thomas is working at the quarry with his friend Mavis the Diesel Engine. During the day, there is a lot going on. People are coming and going, and Thomas and Mavis are kept busy pushing freight cars full of supplies and pulling loads of dirt and stone. It's a lot of hard work, but Thomas likes working with Mavis.

But at night, the quarry is a scary place.

The workers have all gone home, and it is very quiet and dark.

The wind makes funny noises, and the moon makes funny shadows.

Each day seems shorter and colder. Thomas is glad that Mavis is there.

Mavis and Thomas are both excited about Halloween. They like to try to scare each other with stories of ghosts and graveyards.

One night, Thomas was telling Mavis about the Ghost of the Black Loch. Suddenly there was a loud crash.

Both engines were very startled and quite scared. They were looking all around when a raccoon walked out of the trash shed. Thomas peeped loudly. Then it was the raccoon's turn to be startled. Thomas and Mavis laughed.

One morning, the quarry was especially busy.
Everyone was working even harder than usual.
Ropes were being hung from the trees around the
quarry, and tables were being set up everywhere.
And a large pile of wood was being centered in
an even larger circle of stones.

Just then, Thomas' Driver hurried up. "Off we go, Thomas! We are going into Anopha to pick up an important Special."

"What are we picking up?" asked Thomas.

"We have to get the children for the big Halloween party and we don't want to be late."

Thomas was very excited. He couldn't wait to see all of the children in their costumes.

On his way into town, Thomas saw a black cat dart across the tracks and disappear into the bushes on the other side.

"Thomas, did you know it is bad luck if a black cat crosses your tracks?" said his Driver.

"It's not my fault," peeped Thomas. "The cat didn't stop at the crossing signal."

But suddenly Thomas seemed to be having bad luck. As soon as they pulled into Anopha, Thomas had to stop at a crossing so that Gordon could pass with the Express. The train was long, and Gordon was going slower than usual.

Then Thomas had to stop again because someone had left some bags of leaves on the tracks. As his Driver cleared them away, he grumbled, "Some older children think that Halloween is an excuse to do naughty, dangerous things."

And when they finally reached the station, Thomas had to stop behind a big pile of hay and he couldn't see any of the children who were in costume.

To make matters worse, Thomas saw the black
cat again.

"Don't cross my path," Thomas peeped loudly.
"I don't need any more bad luck."

But his luck did not improve. Although
Thomas could hear lots of laughter and voices,
he couldn't see anything going on around him.

"This is terrible," he complained. "I cannot see
a thing."

"No time to chat, Thomas," answered his
Driver. "We have to get back to the quarry—
and fast."

On the way back to the quarry, Thomas had to stop at another signal. This time, it was Bertie who went sailing by.

"*Toot, toot,* slowcoach!" beeped Bertie. "See you there!"

Thomas was very frustrated.

Finally, Thomas chugged into the quarry. As soon as he stopped, children started streaming out of his coaches. They were all in costume as they rushed past Thomas. No one stopped to say hello or show off what they were wearing.

"Sorry, Thomas," said his Driver. "We're a bit late and the children have to hurry to line up for the costume parade. But we are in the perfect spot to see everyone walk by."

Sure enough, soon princesses and ghosts, goblins and pirates, witches and clowns started walking past. Every costume got a round of applause.

Just then, a little girl dressed as a black cat walked by.

"Oh, no!" cried Thomas. "No more bad luck!" But as he was watching the cat go by, he heard a particularly big round of applause and lots of laughter.

"What did I miss? What did I miss?" peeped Thomas. But there was no one left to answer… everyone had moved away; the Halloween party was in full swing.

Thomas looked around. There were people in costume everywhere, bobbing for apples, having their faces painted, drawing pictures.

Thomas wished that he could bob for apples.

He pulled up to Mavis. "Mavis, did you see the last costume? I missed it!"

BOB for PPLES

THE FFARQUHAR QUA

Mavis laughed. "I sure did! And here it comes now!"

Thomas looked over and peeped in surprise.

Coming toward him was a little boy dressed as *him*!

Soon little Thomas was right in front of big Thomas.

"My name is Thomas," said little Thomas, "and you are my favorite engine." And he leaned forward and he gave Thomas a shiny red apple.

Thomas peeped proudly.

And then it was time to light the bonfire.

Everyone watched the large bonfire. There was singing and laughter and Sir Topham Hatt even told a scary story.

"Next year, I would like to dress up," whispered Thomas.

"I think you should dress up as Sir Topham Hatt," teased Mavis.

Thomas and Mavis both laughed and laughed.

Can you find these things in the pictures of this story?